www.makebelieveideas.co.uk

Written by Rosie Greening.
Illustrated by Lara Ede.

This book belongs to

Happy Christmas 2022
from Apple Blossom Playgroup

. . . .

SELFish

Lara Ede ○ Rosie Greening

make
believe
ideas

Back in the days
when **Santa** was small,
he didn't deliver
the **presents** at all.

The **Post Elves** would take
them on scooters they flew.
They hated the work –
it took HOURS to do!

Santa was going to **school** like the rest.
He was **top** of the class and he **aced** every test.

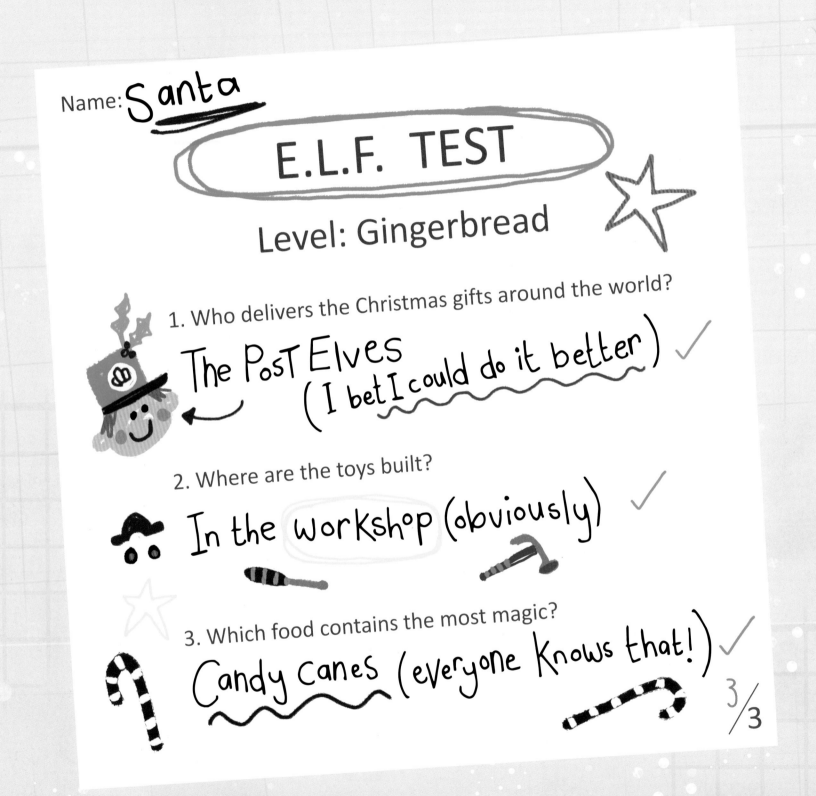

Name: Santa

E.L.F. TEST

Level: Gingerbread

1. Who delivers the Christmas gifts around the world?

The PosT Elves
(I bet I could do it better) ✓

2. Where are the toys built?

In the workshop (obviously) ✓

3. Which food contains the most magic?

Candy canes (everyone knows that!) ✓

3/3

But **Santa** was sadly
a **big-headed** elf.
He was **greedy** and **mean**,
thinking just of **himself**.

He **invented** new toys just for **fun** every day.
When the elves asked to try them, he shouted,

NO WAY!

The teachers despaired,
for Santa had brains.
If only he'd use them
for GOOD, for a change.

One Christmas,
the **Post Elves** rushed in full of fear.

They said,

"We need students
to help us this year!

Our gift list is **long**,
and we're **rushed** off our feet.
We need **stamps** and **addresses**
and **piles** that look **neat**."

The students were **thrilled** to have duties to do.

They **labelled** the **gifts**...

and **piled** them up too.

But **Santa** was grumpy; this **wasn't** his style.
Someone like him should **invent**,
not make piles!

So while all his **classmates** went full steam ahead,
Santa **snuck off** to the **workshop** instead.

"I know how to prove I'm **ELF**tastically skilled!"
He rolled up his sleeves, then he started to **build.**

At last, **Santa** stepped back and saw what he'd done.
He **grinned** to himself, thinking,
"This will be fun!"

One **final thing** would help Santa **succeed.**
He thought,

"The school **stables** have **just** what I need..."

Soon, in the school hall, what should appear
but **Santa,** a **sleigh**
and **eight flying reindeer!**

"I'm awesome!" cried Santa,
and **zoomed** through the air,
forgetting the **big** piles of **gifts** that were there.

CRASH

went the sleigh
and the presents all **fell,**
crushing the scooters
that stood there as well.

"Oh no!" cried the **Post Elves**.

"Today's Christmas Eve. Without gifts or scooters, how can we leave?"

NORTH POLE
EXPRESS
MAIL SERVICE

Santa felt bad as he realised this fact:
he'd just **ruined Christmas**
with one **selfish** act!

But then he remembered the toys in his shed.
"I'll deliver them all in my sleigh!"
Santa said.

The **Post Elves** were thrilled
(they needed a rest).
And **Santa** soon found
that this **job** was the **BEST!**

He loved the **new places** . . .

and **treats** he was fed...

For Santa

but what he **loved** most
was the **joy** that he spread.

From then on, **Santa** gave out the **gifts** every year.
He stopped being selfish and brought **Christmas cheer.**

And he soon made a **list**
(which he always checked twice)
to spread what he'd learnt –
**that it's nice
to be nice!**